caillou®

Sends a Letter

A Chouette Publishing adaptation
Original text by Joceline Sanschagrin, based on the animated series
Illustrations: CINAR Animation

Caillou was
coloring.
His mommy
was singing.
"What a
wonderful
sunny day!"
Mommy said.

"Here's the mail!"
said Mommy.
All sorts of envelopes fell
on top of Gilbert, who
was dozing by the door.
Caillou ran to pick up
the mail.

Mommy opened all the envelopes.
"Nothing but bills. I'd sure like to get a letter once in a while."

"What's the matter, Caillou?" Daddy asked. Caillou explained that Mommy was disappointed with the mail that came every day.

"Mommy would like to get a nice letter."
"Caillou, why don't you send a letter to Mommy?
Your picture would make a wonderful letter!"

Surprised, Caillou looked at the sun he had drawn.
"We could send my picture by mail?"
"Sure, the mailman could deliver it tomorrow
morning," Daddy said.
Caillou thought it was a wonderful idea.

"Now we need an envelope," said Daddy.
"I know where they are, Daddy."
"We'll need a stamp too," Daddy added.

While Caillou was looking for a stamp,
Gilbert walked on the picture lying on the floor.
He left a perfectly clear paw print on it!

"Oh, Gilbert!"
Caillou groaned
when he saw the
paw print.
Caillou heard
Mommy.
"Caillou, where
are you?" she
called.

Caillou quickly
hid his paper under
the table.
"What are you two
up to?" Mommy
asked.
"Nothing at all,"
Daddy replied.
And he winked at
Caillou.

That night, Caillou got his letter ready.
"Tomorrow we'll have to get up very early,"
Daddy said as he slipped the picture into the
envelope.

After he put the stamp on, Caillou looked at his letter. "Wow!" He thought his letter was perfect. Mommy would be very surprised.

The next morning,
Daddy woke
Caillou up very
early. They tiptoed
downstairs and
went out to meet
the mailman.
Caillou gave him
the letter.

Caillou called out, "Mommy, the mailman's coming! Hurry!" Mommy arrived just in time to see all the envelopes land on the floor.
Caillou could hardly stand still while Mommy opened his envelope.

"Oh, Caillou! What a wonderful surprise! Your picture is very beautiful. And you even got Gilbert to sign it!"

"Thank you very much, Caillou. I'll keep this letter forever," Mommy said, giving him a kiss.

"Forever? Wow!" said Caillou.
Mommy was happy. She put Caillou's picture up
on the refrigerator.
"It's the best letter I've ever received!"

A Chouette Publishing adaptation of the original text by Joceline Sanschagrin, based on the
CAILLOU animated film series produced by CINAR Corporation (© 1997 Caillou Productions
Inc., a subsidiary of CINAR Corporation). All rights reserved.
Original scenario written by Thor Bishopric and Todd Swift.
Illustrations taken from the television series CAILLOU.
Graphic design: Monique Dupras
Computer graphics: Les Studios de la Souris Mécanique

Canadian Cataloguing in Publication Data

Sanschagrin, Joceline, 1950-
Caillou sends a letter
New rev. ed.
(Backpack Series)
Translation of: Caillou envoie une lettre
For children aged 3 and up.
Co-published by: CINAR Corporation.

ISBN 2-89450-355-5

1. Postal service - Juvenile literature.   2. Letter writing - Juvenile literature.
I. CINAR Corporation. II. Title. III. Series.

HE6076.S2613 2002   j383   C2002-941168-6

Legal deposit: 2002

We gratefully acknowledge the financial support of BPIDP and SODEC
for our publishing activities.

Printed in China
10 9 8 7 6 5 4 3 2 1